Over eighty years have passed since The Hound of the Baskervilles *was first published, and it is still one of the most gripping mystery stories ever written. Its hero is the great detective Sherlock Holmes, whose deductive powers are famous. Some of the methods used by Sherlock Holmes were later adopted by criminal investigation departments throughout the world.*

First Edition

© LADYBIRD BOOKS LTD MCMLXXXII

THE HOUND OF THE BASKERVILLES

by Sir Arthur Conan Doyle

retold in simple language
by Raymond Sibley

illustrated by Drury Lane Studios

Ladybird Books Loughborough

The Hound of the Baskervilles

My friend Sherlock Holmes was involved in some very unusual cases of detection, but never one as strange as that I am about to tell.

It began ordinarily enough one morning in late September 1890, at his London flat in Baker Street. Holmes had in his hand a faded yellow document of some age, for it was dated 'Baskerville Hall 1742'. He told me that it had been left for him to look at by a James Mortimer. 'Like you, Watson,' said Holmes, 'he is a doctor, and he is calling on me in person later this morning.' The faded parchment told of the curse on the Baskerville family and how it had begun . . . .

Long ago, Baskerville Hall on the edge of the Devon Moor had been held by Sir Hugo Baskerville, a wild and cruel man. Sir Hugo had taken a fancy to the daughter of a farmer who lived across the moor a few miles from the Baskerville estate. The girl however was afraid of Hugo for she knew of his bad character, and would have nothing to do with him.

One bleak afternoon, when the girl's father and brothers were away from their farm, Hugo and some of his friends kidnapped her. They took her to Baskerville Hall and locked her in an upstairs room. During the evening the sounds of singing and shouting from Hugo and his drunken companions in the hall below terrified her. She opened the window, climbed down the ivy on the stone wall and started to run across the moonlit moor towards her home.

When Hugo found she had escaped he was filled with rage. He shouted that he would give his body and soul to the Powers of Evil if he could recapture the maid, and his drunken followers shrank from him in horror.

Hugo rushed to the stables, set loose his pack of hounds, mounted his horse and galloped wildly after the girl.

After a time his friends found their courage once more. Several of them fetched their horses and rode after Hugo, hoping that they would be in time to save the girl.

When they had gone a mile or two they met a night shepherd on the moorlands. The man was almost too shocked to speak, but he told them, 'Hugo Baskerville passed me on his mare, and behind him ran an enormous black hound of hell.'

On they went. Soon they heard the sound of galloping, and Hugo's mare came alone out of the night, its mouth dabbled with froth and its saddle empty.

Now they rode close together, for a great fear was on them. At the entrance to a clearing they found the hounds huddled together, shivering with terror.

In the middle of the clearing lay the dead body of the girl. Lying near her was Hugo Baskerville, and over him stood a great black beast, shaped like a hound. As the horsemen watched, it tore the throat out of its victim, then turned its blazing eyes and dripping jaws on them. They turned and fled, shrieking, across the moor.

Ever since that night the Baskerville Curse has passed from father to son. Many have died violent and mysterious deaths and those who are to come are warned never to cross the moor alone in those dark hours when the devil hound is about. Here the document ended.

When Dr Mortimer arrived, Holmes gave him back the manuscript and said that he did not concern himself with fairy tales.

'Be patient, Mr Holmes,' replied Mortimer. 'It is important that you know the contents of the document before I tell you details of the death of the last of the Baskervilles: my friend Sir Charles, just three months ago.' He went on to tell us that Sir Charles' behaviour, in the weeks before his death, had been very odd. Sir Charles was convinced that the curse of the hound was upon him. He dared not go on the moor at night. Often he had asked Mortimer whether he had seen any strange creatures or heard the baying of a hound. Mortimer felt that in addition to his heart trouble Sir Charles was straining his nervous system to breaking point. He had also become a man of habit. Every night he walked from Baskerville Hall along the gravel drive to the moor gate, but he would never go any further.

One night in June, his body was found near the moor gate by his butler, Barrymore. The soft gravel drive showed two sets of footprints: those of Sir Charles and Barrymore. Towards the spot where Sir Charles had died, it seemed that he had started to walk on his toes.

'I was sent for,' continued Dr Mortimer. 'I examined the body. It had no physical injuries on it, but the face was twisted with terror. He had died from heart failure. Barrymore told me that there were no marks on the ground around

the body but I saw some about twenty yards away, on the grass, before they were destroyed by the steady rain.'

Holmes looked at Mortimer with a hard glitter of interest in his eyes. 'Were they footprints?'

'Yes.'

'A man's or a woman's?'

Dr Mortimer looked at us in a curious way, and his voice sank to a whisper as he answered, 'Mr Holmes, they were the footprints of a gigantic hound.'

At these words a shudder went through me.

Holmes looked at him. 'What exactly have you come to see me about, Dr Mortimer?'

'I want you to advise me. In one hour Sir Henry Baskerville arrives in London from Canada. He is the son of Sir Charles' younger brother, and the last of the Baskervilles.' Dr Mortimer added that the only other Baskerville, Rodger, had died in Brazil of yellow fever some years before. Rodger was descended from Sir Hugo of the legend.

'In your opinion, Mr Holmes, is Dartmoor a safe place for a Baskerville? We want Sir Henry to live among us and carry on the good work his uncle, Sir Charles, did for the poor of the district.'

'My advice is to meet Sir Henry and bring him to see me this afternoon. Just one more question: several people saw a hound on the moor before Sir Charles' death, but have any seen it since?'

'No, Mr Holmes.'

When Dr Mortimer had gone, I asked Holmes why Sir Charles had walked on tiptoe down the gravel path. 'That's nonsense, Watson. He was running for his life. But running from what? That's our problem.'

Now we awaited the arrival of Sir Henry Baskerville. In the middle of the afternoon Dr Mortimer returned with him. He was a pleasant,

strongly built man of about thirty.

Sir Henry listened carefully as Dr Mortimer told him all the details of the Baskerville Curse. Then he said quietly, but firmly, that there was no devil in Hell and no man on earth who could stop him going to Baskerville Hall. 'Good. That settles the matter,' said Holmes, 'but Watson must go with you.'

The next day Sir Henry, Dr Mortimer and I, travelled to Devon by train. Holmes had to stay in London for a few days on an important case. The journey was a pleasant one and, as we talked, I formed a great liking for both Sir Henry and Dr Mortimer.

When we reached the small village station in Devon, an open carriage pulled by two horses awaited us. Soon the driver was taking us through the evening twilight to the edge of the moor. It rose up in front of us in the sinking sun, and a cold wind sweeping across it made us shiver. The grim wasteland, the chill wind and the darkening sky made us silent. In front of us were rocks, wild scenery and twisted trees.

Suddenly the driver pointed with his whip and said, 'Baskerville Hall.' A few minutes later we had reached the lodge gates. We passed into a private road bordered by trees, with Baskerville Hall glimmering like a ghost at the other end.

The butler, Barrymore, stepped from the porch to welcome us, then the driver went on to take Dr Mortimer home.

Inside, the house was a place of shadow and gloom. 'It isn't very cheerful,' said Sir Henry. We had a meal and then went straight to bed. When I looked out from my bedroom window over the moor, it seemed cold, grey and unfriendly. In the deathly silence of the old house, I lay for some time before sleep came.

When Sir Henry and I sat at breakfast next morning, with the sunlight streaming through the windows, our spirits were much higher. After breakfast Sir Henry had some business to attend to, so I took a walk along the edge of the moor. I had gone two or three miles, when someone called my name. It was a man between thirty and forty and he was carrying a butterfly net and a tin specimen box.

He introduced himself as Jack Stapleton. His friend Dr Mortimer had told him about me. 'I love the moor,' he said, 'but I have only lived here for two years.'

As he spoke a dreadful cry of agony echoed across the moor. It turned me cold with horror. Stapleton's nerves seemed stronger than mine for he said calmly, 'It's a moor pony caught in the Grimpen Marsh.' I looked into the distance and saw the pony being gradually sucked down. Its neck rolled and twitched for some time, as it slowly disappeared.

'It's a bad place, the Grimpen Marsh,' said Stapleton, quietly. 'I know my way through it, to where the rare butterflies are, but take my advice and keep away from it.' Nothing moved, apart from two ravens on a rock behind us. Then a very long moaning sound swept the moor and died away. 'Good God!' I said. 'What was that?'

Stapleton looked at me with a strange expression. 'They say it is the hound of the Baskervilles calling for its prey. I've heard it before, but never so loud.' I looked around with a chill of fear in my heart. Stapleton seemed unmoved and after saying that he would like to meet Sir Henry, he walked off towards the old farmhouse where he lived.

The death of the pony, and the curious sound like a hound, had upset me. I returned to Baskerville Hall with my head full of vague fears.

Next day Stapleton called. He took Sir Henry and me on the moor, and he showed us the spot where the legend said that the wicked Hugo had died. It was a dismal place. Stapleton seemed very eager to be friendly with Sir Henry.

On the following day Sir Henry and I walked to the nearby village of Grimpen. We stayed at Dr Mortimer's house for some time, talking, and it was twilight before we started home along the moor path. As darkness fell Sir Henry said jokingly that the legend warned all Baskervilles never to cross the moor at night. As if in answer to his words, there arose out of the gloom that same strange cry I had heard with Stapleton. 'Good heavens, Watson! That was a hound!' From the break in his voice I could tell he was frightened. 'It's one thing to laugh about it in London, Watson, and another to stand out here in the darkness of the moor and hear that cry. I feel very cold. Am I really in danger?'

Immediately I began to hurry him back to Baskerville Hall. As we walked I glanced upwards. Some distance away was a large rock and standing on it, outlined in black against the sky, was the figure of a man, watching us. With a cry of surprise I pointed him out to Sir Henry. In the moment it took for Sir Henry to turn his head, the man had disappeared. But I was not mistaken. I had seen him, and I was soon to have proof of this from Barrymore.

When we reached Baskerville Hall, I found Barrymore waiting for me. He said that a man was in hiding on the moor, living in one of the empty stone cottages. I asked him how he knew that and he replied that one of the village boys went daily to the stranger, taking food.

Barrymore was upset. He said that the moor was frightening enough without a stranger hiding and watching at night. It seemed that Barrymore and I were both thinking along the same lines. Had the stranger anything to do with the hound? We were both worried for Sir Henry's safety.

I decided what to do. The following afternoon I went out straight after lunch, taking my revolver with me. Slowly I crossed the moor in the direction of Black Tor, where the stone cottages were. I searched each in turn until in one of them I found some blankets, a bucket of water, some empty tins, food and a bottle of brandy. I was certain I had tracked down the stranger's hiding place.

It was mid-afternoon. I sat down to wait, with my revolver handy. About an hour had passed when I heard someone coming. I got into the darkest corner and held the pistol ready, with my finger on the trigger.

Whoever it was stopped outside the open doorway. There was a long pause. Then a voice said, 'Why don't you come outside, Watson? It's a beautiful evening!' For a moment I was hardly able to believe my ears.

'Holmes!' I cried.

'Come out,' he said, 'and be careful with that pistol!'

I was overjoyed to see him. He told me he had wanted everyone, including myself, to think he was in London. In fact, he had followed us to Devon by the train after ours. Then he had gone into hiding on the moor, so that he could watch and wait.

Holmes questioned me about where I had been, what I had done and who I had met. He listened carefully and when I mentioned Stapleton, Holmes said that he was not the harmless person he pretended to be.

'What do you mean?' I asked.

'Behind that smiling, friendly face he is calmly plotting murder,' said Holmes. 'Cold-blooded and deliberate murder. I can't explain the details now. My plans are closing in on him, just as his are on Sir Henry. The only danger is that he will strike first. In a day or so my case against him will be complete.'

He said there was now no longer any need for him to remain in hiding, and we went back together to Baskerville Hall. Sir Henry was very pleased to see Sherlock Holmes. 'How is the case going, Mr Holmes? Have you made any sense of it yet?' Holmes said the matter would be solved before very long, if when the time came, Sir Henry would do exactly what he was told to do, without argument. To this Sir Henry agreed. Then he went to his room.

Once he had gone, Holmes and I went to the dining-hall. On the walls hung paintings of the Baskervilles going back over three hundred years. Holmes moved from painting to painting, looking very carefully at each in turn. Then he went back and held a lamp to one in particular,

studying it closely. It was a portrait of a man in black velvet and lace — the wicked Sir Hugo who had started it all.

'Look at it, Watson.'

I did so. I noticed the thin-lipped mouth, the cold eye and the stern expression.

'Now look again!' said Holmes.

He stood on a chair and put his hand over the broad hat and the curling hair, so that only the face was visible.

I started in surprise. The likeness between the face of Sir Hugo and the man we knew as Stapleton was almost beyond belief. 'It looks like Stapleton!' I said.

Holmes laughed. 'Yes, Stapleton must have Baskerville blood in him. Now we can guess why he is an enemy to Sir Henry. Never mind, tomorrow night I shall trap him. Not a word of this to Sir Henry.'

Holmes was up early in the morning and seemed to be in good spirits. Sir Henry had been invited to visit Stapleton that evening. He asked Holmes and myself if we would like to go with him. 'I'm afraid not,' said Holmes. 'You will have to go alone, as Watson and I must be in London on important business.'

This was news to me, but I said nothing. Sir Henry looked disappointed. 'I would like to go to London with you.'

'You must stay here,' said Holmes. 'Remember you promised to carry out all my instructions without question. I want you to go to your friend Stapleton's tonight, as planned. Afterwards you are to walk home by the path across the moor. Tell Stapleton you intend to do this.'

'But that's the very thing you have told me never to do,' replied Sir Henry.

'Trust me,' insisted Holmes. 'This time you may do it with safety. It will take great courage. You must not stray away from the moor path leading from Stapleton's house to Grimpen village. Keep on that path at all costs.' I was as puzzled by all this as was Sir Henry, but I kept quiet.

A couple of hours later we left Baskerville Hall for the railway station. At the platform Holmes dismissed the carriage driver. When the driver was out of sight he told me we were not going anywhere. Part of his plan was to let Stapleton believe we were in London, so that he would then feel safe to attack Sir Henry. This was exactly what Holmes wanted him to do. I was not completely surprised. Sherlock Holmes rarely told his full plans to anyone, including myself.

We had a meal and talked more about
Stapleton. Holmes had photographs, copies of
statements from witnesses and various
documents. They proved that Stapleton had
lived under different names, in different parts of
England, for some time.

After the meal Holmes hired a driver and
carriage. He had still not told me what we were
to do or what we were to expect. Off we drove
in the darkness. The presence of the driver
meant we could not talk openly. I could feel my
heart beating when we were back on the moor.

The driver put us down near to Baskerville Hall, and we turned in the direction of Stapleton's house and began to walk. It seemed a long way. Over towards Grimpen Marsh lay a huge bank of fog. Holmes stopped about two hundred yards from the house. 'This will do,' he said. 'These rocks will give us cover.'

We got into a hollow behind the rocks, but although we could see the house, we were too far away to see what was happening inside.

After some minutes Holmes asked me to creep forward to see what Sir Henry and Stapleton were doing, and I tiptoed to the low orchard wall. At one place I could see through the uncurtained window into the room where they were dining.

Stapleton was talking. Sir Henry looked pale.
Perhaps the thought of that lonely walk back
across the moor was on his mind.

As I watched, Stapleton left the room. He
came outside and went into an outhouse. I
heard a curious scuffling noise, then after a
minute or so he came out, locked the door and
returned to Sir Henry. I crept back and reported
to Holmes what I had seen.

By this time, the bank of fog over Grimpen Marsh had begun drifting in our direction. 'This is serious, Watson. It's moving towards us. Sir Henry must leave before the fog reaches the path. His life depends on it. He can't be long now, it's already after ten.'

Every minute we waited, the fog drifted closer. The first thin wisps had reached the farthest wall of Stapleton's orchard. Slowly it crept around the trees. 'If he doesn't come soon, we shall lose him,' said Holmes.

'We must move back a little onto higher ground.' Still the fog swept slowly on. Holmes knelt down and put his ear to the ground. 'I think I can hear him coming.'

Then I heard him too. We crouched down among the rocks staring hard into the fog as the footsteps grew louder. Sir Henry came out of the fog, walking swiftly. He passed us. Every now and then he looked behind him, like a frightened man.

'Watson!' cried Holmes. 'It's coming.'

About fifty yards from where we were a
dreadful shape burst out of the fog. I sprang to
my feet. It was a hound; an enormous black
hound. Light seemed to come from its mouth
and flicker around its eyes and jaws. Never
have I seen anything so hellish. With long
bounds it followed hard on the track of our

friend, Sir Henry. We were so shocked we let it pass us before we recovered our nerves. Then Holmes and I fired together. It gave a howl of pain, but did not stop.

Sir Henry had turned and was looking in helpless terror at the thing which was hunting him down.

But the cry of pain from the hound had told us that it was a living thing, and not a ghost-dog. Holmes ran after the hound. We heard the screams of Sir Henry. The beast had hurled him to the ground and was about to attack his throat. Holmes put five shots from his revolver into the creature. It rolled over on to its back,

pawed the air and then fell still. I stooped over it, with my pistol drawn, but the giant hound was dead.

Sir Henry had fainted. His eyelids quivered. I gave him some brandy from my flask.

'My God!' he whispered. 'What was it?'

'Whatever it was, it is dead,' said Holmes. 'The family ghost has been killed for ever.'

The size of the creature was huge. It was neither pure bloodhound, nor pure mastiff, but a mixture of the two, and as large as a small lioness. The head and jaws seemed to glow with a bluish light. I put my hand on its head, and as I lifted my fingers they too gleamed blue in the darkness.

'Phosphorus,' I said.

'A clever preparation of it,' replied Holmes.

We knew that the sound of the shots must have warned Stapleton that the game was up. The three of us went to his house and searched it room by room, but our quarry had gone. Holmes had planned well, for Stapleton's only escape route was through Grimpen Marsh. Since it would have been useless to try to find him in the fog, we returned to Baskerville Hall. On the way, Sherlock Holmes told Sir Henry how Stapleton had plotted to kill him.

On the morning after the death of the hound, the fog lifted and Dr Mortimer guided us to a pathway through Grimpen Marsh. The rotting reeds and slimy water-plants gave off a smell of decay, and several times we sank thigh-deep into the quivering mud.

We saw traces that someone had passed that way before us. Further on we found Stapleton's hat, lost by him the night before in his flight through the fog. That was the last sign we saw of him. If the earth told a true story, somewhere in the heart of Grimpen Marsh, sucked down in the foul slime, Stapleton was buried for ever.

In an old hut, where Stapleton had kept the hound, we found a very strong chain, a pile of gnawed bones and a tin containing the paste mixture used on the creature's head and jaws, to make it appear ghostly. This must certainly have helped to frighten Sir Charles to death.

Stapleton had not dared to keep the hound at his house, except on the nights of the attacks on Sir Charles and Sir Henry. He had kept it hidden, but he could not quieten its voice.

There were still many points which I did not understand. Some days later, on the train back to London, Holmes explained.

Stapleton was indeed a Baskerville. This was something we had not expected, for Dr Mortimer had told us in the beginning that Sir Henry was the last of the Baskervilles.

It was not so. Rodger, the brother of Sir Charles, had not died of yellow fever in Brazil. In fact he had married and had one son, also called Rodger. That son we knew later under the name of Stapleton.

When Stapleton came to England he found out that only one or two lives stood between him and the rich estate of Baskerville.

To begin with, his plans were vague. His first act was to live near to Baskerville Hall. His second was to become friendly with Sir Charles.

When Sir Charles told him the story of the Baskerville curse, Stapleton thought of a way to make it come true. From another friend, Dr Mortimer, he had learned that Sir Charles had a weak heart, and that any violent shock would kill him.

He bought the dog in London, from dealers in the Fulham Road. It was the strongest, biggest and most savage animal they could find.

No one knows how many times Stapleton waited with the hound in the darkness without success. Then one night, as Sir Charles strolled along the drive, Stapleton released his hound. Sir Charles ran in terror and his heart failed. Stapleton called off the hound and took it back to its hut on Grimpen Marsh.

It is just possible that Stapleton did not know then of another Baskerville living in Canada. If so, he must have had a shock himself when he learned of Sir Henry. It meant he had to plan another death.

By the time Holmes was found by me, when he was in hiding on the moor, he had worked out most of the case against Stapleton. He knew also that he would have to catch Stapleton in the act, for nothing could be proved against him. So Sir Henry had to be used as bait, to make Stapleton act.

50

One thing still puzzled me. If Sir Henry had been killed, how could Stapleton have claimed the Baskerville title without giving himself away? He had lived in the district for two years under a false name and there would have been two strange deaths.

Even Holmes had no real answer to this. It is likely that Stapleton would have returned quietly to Brazil and claimed the Baskerville fortune from there under his real name, Rodger Baskerville. By doing so he would have had no need to come to England at all.

Only one thing is certain: that cruel and evil man would have tried to find a way.

Stories . . . that have stood the test of time

Ladybird titles cover a wide range of subjects and reading ages.
Write for a free illustrated list from the publishers:
LADYBIRD BOOKS LTD Loughborough Leicestershire England